John A. Stevens

The Burgoyne Campaign

an address delivered on the battle-field on the one hundredth celebration

of the Battle of Bemis Heights, September 19, 1877

John A. Stevens

The Burgoyne Campaign
*an address delivered on the battle-field on the one hundredth celebration of the
Battle of Bemis Heights, September 19, 1877*

ISBN/EAN: 9783337390273

Printed in Europe, USA, Canada, Australia, Japan

Cover: Foto ©Andreas Hilbeck / pixelio.de

More available books at **www.hansebooks.com**

THE BURGOYNE CAMPAIGN

AN ADDRESS

DELIVERED ON THE BATTLE-FIELD

ON THE

ONE HUNDREDTH CELEBRATION

OF THE

BATTLE OF BEMIS HEIGHTS

SEPTEMBER 19, 1877

BY

JOHN AUSTIN STEVENS,

––––––––

NEW YORK
ANSON D. F. RANDOLPH & COMPANY
900 BROADWAY
1877.

THE BURGOYNE CAMPAIGN

MR. CHAIRMAN, CITIZENS OF SARATOGA COUNTY,
LADIES AND GENTLEMEN :

To appear before you on this interesting occasion, com-
memorative of an important event in the annals of the State and
country, is to me not only a signal honor and a grateful task
but a filial duty.   Proud to be chosen to recite the incidents
of the campaign which culminated in the surrender of the first
British army to the infant republic, it is a source of still
greater pride to me that I am thus permitted to link my own
name in the chain of history with that of my grandfather,
Col. Ebenezer Stevens, of the Continental army, who, on this
field, a century ago, directed, as Major Commandant of the
Artillery of the Northern Department, the operations of that
arm of the service which in great measure contributed to and
secured the final success of the American troops.

The ground on which we stand is memorable.   Before the
discovery of the continent, this territory, at whose southern
angle we are now gathered, was the battle-field of the Indian
tribes, whose war trails lay upon its boundaries, and from the
days of European settlement it has been the debatable ground
of the French and Dutch, the French and English, and the
colonists and English, by turns.   Here the fate of American empire has been repeatedly sealed.   Not because of its
matchless beauty of hill and dale, its mirrored lakes and crys-
tal streams, its invigorating atmosphere and perfect skies,

nor yet because of its unmeasured forests and fertile fields, was this old territory of Saratoga and Kayaderosseras the object of rivalry and contention. Its possession was of supreme military importance. The Mohawk pours into the Hudson at its southernmost limit ; its borders are protected by their waters, while a series of declivities, descending from the mountain ranges of Luzerne and Kayaderosseras and terminating in groups of isolated hills, present an admirable strategic point. The discovery of Lake Champlain in 1609, by the brave Frenchman whose name it bears, and the sailing up the Hudson by Henry Hudson, the same year, gave rise to a contest for its possession between the Canadian and New York colonists which lasted for more than a century and a half.

The French settlements spread rapidly up the St. Lawrence and far into the western country, while the Dutch and English slowly and methodically pushed their way along the Hudson, and thence by the Mohawk to the great interior lakes. From the mouth of the Mohawk, northward, skirting the shores of the Hudson and the lakes, lay the highway between the rival settlements and posts. In its route it passed the carrying-places of the Indians. Over this road, then but an Indian trail, the troops of Frontenac passed in 1693, on their way to strike the fortified villages of the Mohawk. Upon it Colonel Schuyler built the forts from Stillwater to Fort Ann, in the war of 1709.

In the campaigns of 1744 and 1755, the French and their Indian allies, with war-whoop, scalping-knife and tomahawk, swept down through the forests to the settlements of this region ; and in the seven years' war that followed, from 1755 to 1763, it was by this road that Abercrombie led his troops to defeat and Amherst to the final triumph of the English arms ; and here again swept back and forth the tide of war in alternate ebb and flow during the earlier period of the American Revolution.

In the beginning of the contest the spirit of the colonies was little understood in England. Notwithstanding the warning of the American agents, it was believed that the war would be localized in Massachusetts, and that General Gage and a few regiments would easily reduce the rebellious colony. The uprising of the continent in reply to the guns at Lexington dispelled this illusion, and the British Ministry awakening to the magnitude of their undertaking, plans were laid for a continental campaign.

Here a protest may be pardoned against the assumption of those who have doubted the ability of the colonies to maintain the liberty they had asserted without the French intervention, which the victory of Saratoga secured to the American cause. A careful examination of the letters and newspapers of the day, which, in the words of Webster, are the only true sources of historic information, will show that the colonists never doubted of their cause, and that they knew the reason of the faith that was in them. They were fully aware of the numbers they had contributed to the British forces in the Canadian conquest, and of the prowess they had displayed side by side with the best of the British regiments.

They were also informed of the extreme difficulty with which the home Government obtained its recruits. Already in the middle of the last century, under the atrocious land system of England and the development of manufactures, the agricultural population, the yeomanry, hardy sons of the soil, which is the base of every great military state, had been fast disappearing. It was in 1770, before the Revolution, that Goldsmith, the poet of the people, breathed his lament over the happy days long past—

> " Ere England's grief began,
> When every rood of land maintained its man."

The words of the poet were as familiar to Americans as to their English parents, and they had received a striking confirmation in the enlistment by the Ministry of Hessian mercenaries, whose appearance in the colonies, while exciting the indignation of the patriots, was positive proof of the unpopularity of the war in England and the weakness of the mother country.

The earlier movements of the colonial leaders show that they were thoroughly acquainted with the art of war in its larger sense. They recognized the value of the great lines of water communication—the St. Lawrence and the Hudson—and foresaw that the first efforts of the British Ministry would be to control their mouths, from which, by their superior naval power, they could force the passages of the rivers and divide the territory. The Northern and Eastern people recognized this intuitively, and gave point and direction to the movement toward Canada by the seizure of Ticonderoga and Crown Point at the outset of hostilities. These important posts were surprised by the Eastern militia. Their artillery and stores were of priceless value to the Continental cause.

The road to the St. Lawrence thus opened, and the temper of the Canadians and Indians of the lower provinces favoring the undertaking, it was resolved by Congress, in June, 1775, to take possession of St. John and Montreal, and General Schuyler was intrusted with the command of the forces destined for that purpose. No appointment could have been more appropriate than this. A gentleman of large landed estate in the northern section, thoroughly conversant with its resources and topography, and familiar not only with the habits and customs of the frontier population, but also wielding a great personal influence with the Indian tribes, he was the only man who could effectually neutralize the efforts of the British agents to influence the savages, who had always taken an active part in the border warfare. Moreover, his great wealth and family alliances gave strength to the cause. Selecting Ticonderoga as his natural base of operations, Schuyler built boats for a movement to surprise St. John, a position so important that it was called by the British officers the key of Canada.

It is not possible here to recount the various incidents of the campaign. On the 3d of November, 1775, after a siege of fifty days, the garrison at St. John capitulated to Montgomery, whom Schuyler, forced by illness, contracted in the wet, unhealthy country, to return to Ticonderoga, had left in command. On the 12th Montgomery was at Montreal. Meanwhile, Washington, to create a diversion in favor of the main movement, had sent Arnold by the way of the Kennebec and the Chaudière to a direct attack on Quebec. After incredible hardships, in the midst of a winter remarkable for its inclemency, Arnold reached Point Levi, opposite Quebec, on the 10th November. The junction of Montgomery and Arnold was made on the 3d December.

On the morning of the last day of the year the assault was made ; the Americans were repulsed, and Montgomery fell. Thus ended the offensive movement upon Canada. Its result was the permanent holding by the British of the post of Quebec—which became impregnable with the reinforcements received from England—and the mouth of the St. Lawrence, for a naval movement toward the lakes. In the beginning of 1776 efforts were made to strengthen the American force in Canada ; and the old road by the riverside, from Albany through Stillwater and Saratoga, was again trodden by thousands of recruits, marching to almost certain death by battle or disease. Upon the death of Montgomery the command of the army before Quebec devolved on Wooster. He was superseded by Thomas in May. The small-pox was raging. To convey an idea of the extent to which it had ravaged the army, it is only necessary to state that, on taking command, Thomas found that of 1,900 men and officers 900 were sick, chiefly with this disease. A retreat was ordered, but the reinforced garrison sallying suddenly forth, the artillery was abandoned, and the Americans fled in precipitation. In June Thomas died of the small-pox at Chamblee, leaving Sullivan in command. An attempt by the new chief to arrest the retreat was the cause of further disaster. Thompson, who led an expedition against Three Rivers, fell into an ambuscade, and was defeated by General Fraser. Among the British troops engaged were some who, arrived from England with the reinforcements under Burgoyne, had been piloted past Quebec by the orders of the sagacious Carleton in the very transports that had conveyed them across the ocean, and pushed up the river to the scene of action. Already the vast importance of the river as a means of military communication was apparent. The remainder of the fleet with the British reinforcements coming up, the post of Sorel was abandoned by the Americans and the retreat again began. So close was the pursuit that the British advance entered Chamblee as the American rear left the town. At St. John they were joined by Arnold from Montreal. Firing the city, they again fell back to Isle aux Noix, and thence, slowly pursued by Burgoyne, to Crown Point, which they reached in the last days of June. [1776.]

So ended the invasion of Canada, an expedition remarkable for its display of human suffering, human energy, and human endurance. History may be searched in vain for examples of greater pertinacity under disaster, greater vigor under the severest trials. The fragments of the gallant bands which had united before Quebec and were now huddled together at Crown Point presented a picture which wrung the stoutest hearts. Pestilence was in their countenances. Pestilence infested the very air ; not a tent in which there was not a dead or dying man. The bones of the heroic Montgomery and his aide-de-camp, McPherson, lay within the walls of Quebec ; Burr and Lamb were prisoners ; Arnold still chafed under a painful wound, and the army itself had dwindled to a handful of emaciated skeletons. The troops at Crown Point now fell under the authority of General Schuyler. From the beginning the ill-health of Schuyler had rendered it impossible for him to take the field at the head of the army; moreover, his great organizing spirit, his tireless energy, were of more service to the cause at the Albany headquarters, where his encouraging presence was indispensable.   .

Arnold arrived at Albany with news of the retreat from Canada on the 24th of June. The next day Schuyler received information of the appointment of Major-General Gates to the command of the forces in Canada.

The instructions to Gates gave him unusual powers. A question of jurisdiction at once arose, however, between himself and Schuyler, which they agreed to submit to Congress, which on the 8th determined it by leaving the supreme authority to Schuyler while this side of Canada, and to Gates when on the other side of the line.

Horatio Gates, who now first appears upon the scene on the Canadian frontier, was of English birth. The son of a clergyman, he received his name from his godfather, Horace Walpole, under whose protection he early entered the British service, and rose rapidly to the rank of major. His regiment being ordered to America, he was badly wounded in the Braddock campaign. Later he distinguished himself by his bravery and capacity as an aide to Monckton on the expedition against Martinique. At the close of the French war he purchased a fine estate in Berkeley County, Va., and became a successful farmer. On the breaking out of the Revolution he volunteered his services to Congress, and receiving the rank of brigadier, was chosen adjutant-general of the army. In this capacity his military experience and training were of great value in the organization of the Continental forces, and he was thus engaged in daily communication with General Washington when he was assigned to his new command. He had been elected by Congress to the rank of major-general in May.

Sullivan, taking offence at Gates' appointment, had retired from the army at Crown Point, the command of which was now assumed by Gates. A council of war, at which Schuyler, Gates, Sullivan, Arnold, and Baron de Woedtke were present, considering Crown Point as not tenable, ordered a withdrawal to Ticonderoga, which was effected. This gave great umbrage to Colonel Stark and other New England officers, who remonstrated with Schuyler against the move. The council which ordered the withdrawal also resolved upon the defence of Lake Champlain, by a naval armament of gondolas, row galleys, and armed batteaux.

On the 16th of July Gates reported that the loss sustained by death and desertion during the campaign amounted to more than five thousand men, and that three thousand more were sick. The army gradually recovered its health and spirits, the defences of Ticonderoga and Mount Independence

were strengthened, connection was made between the camp
and the road to Skenesborough, guns were mounted, and, in
a word, every endeavor made to secure the northern gateway
of the New York colony.   Though a further offensive movement against Canada seemed no longer practicable, the line
of the Hudson and the lakes was of paramount importance.
While all eyes were turned in this direction, danger suddenly
appeared at the other end of the line.   New York City was
invested by the most powerful fleet that had ever appeared
in these western waters, and Washington was threatened by
Lord Howe with a force of thirty thousand men.   In July,
Long Island was occupied by the enemy ; in September, New
York fell into their permanent possession, and Washington
retreated to the mainland.

The naval armament prepared for the defence of Lake
Champlain, by Arnold and the Americans, with incredible
patience and labor, consisted of eight gondolas, three row galleys, and four sloops or schooners, but when finished there were
only landsmen to command and soldiers to manœuvre them.
Arnold, it is true, had gained some experience as a super-
cargo on West India voyages ; yet, with his usual careless
imprudence, he left the main channel of Lake Champlain free,
and on the 4th of October sailed into the open lake.   Meanwhile Carleton, assisted by shipbuilders from England, with
abundant material from the Admiralty and the fleet on the
Canadian stations, had constructed more than two hundred
flat-boats at Montreal, and hauled them to St. John, where
they were launched and manned by seven hundred sailors and
picked officers from the ships-of-war and a large force of German sharpshooters and light artillery trained for the special
service.   On the 11th he sailed into the lake, and taking
the main passage which Arnold had left open, fell on the
American rear.   A sharp action ensued, and for two days
a running fight was maintained.   Arnold's vessel sustained
the contest to the last, but was finally driven into a creek
on the eastern shore, where she was fired, the crew marching
away in perfect order, with colors flying.

On the 14th Carleton landed at Crown Point, the master of the lake. Two hours distant lay Ticonderoga, an easy prey. But further movement was not his intention. He returned to Canada, and went into winter quarters in November. Thus was the golden opportunity lost for a junction of his forces with those of Lord Howe. This military blunder must not be ascribed to Carleton, who had received explicit instructions from Lord Germain to return to Quebec and re-establish good order and government in the province. He was also directed to send a detachment, under Burgoyne or some other officer, to reinforce General Howe at New York. When Gates heard that Carleton had turned his back on Crown Point he dismissed the militia, which had rallied in large numbers to his support. He had no provisions for their maintenance, and no ammunition for an offensive movement, had such a movement been desirable. The season of 1776 closed with Quebec and New York in the hands of the British. The lines of invasion by the St. Lawrence and lower Hudson were entirely open to the enemy. Schuyler was at Albany, indefatigable in his labors to secure the northern defences, and Washington in the Jerseys, covering the Highlands, and ready to move on any menaced point.

Having thus endeavored as hurriedly as possible to sketch the Canada campaign from its promising beginning to its disastrous close, a few words may be permitted before passing to the consideration of the events of 1777, which we are to-day celebrating, as to the attitude and position of New York at this juncture. For both the offensive campaign of 1776 and the defensive campaign of 1777 Northern New York, with Albany as its centre, was the base of operations. It was the Albany Committee of Safety which first garrisoned Ticonderoga after its capture. At Albany, arms, ammunition, and supplies were gathered. There guns were mounted, ammunition fixed, cartridges prepared. The magazines, arsenals, and laboratories were there. Till the final peace in 1783, Albany was not only the secure base for all the operations of the Northern Department, but the supply point whence the material of war was drawn even for distant expeditions.

Unfortunately for the perfect fame of our great State, justice has never yet been done to its history. The Dutch period has been admirably portrayed by O'Callaghan and Broadhead, but the recital of her struggle for liberty and independence through the whole of the eighteenth century yet awaits the pen of some one of her gifted sons. When it shall be written, it will be found that she was second to none in devotion to the principles of individual freedom, not for herself alone, but for all the colonies. Her first commercial corporation displayed this feeling in the adoption of the generous motto : " *Non nobis nati solum* "—we are not born for ourselves alone, and during her subsequent history this has been her marked characteristic.

Her central position made her the seat of war and subjected her to privations and sufferings which were unknown to the other colonies. Indeed, her calamities were a source of profit to her Eastern neighbors. When New York flourished they participated in her commerce and shared her prosperity, but when by the fortune of war her opulent seaport fell into the hands of the enemy, she was not only burdened by a large population which had depended upon the luxury and trade of the capital, but, by an unjust customs discrimination, was compelled to pay tribute to neighboring colonies, who refused to permit the passage through their territory of goods intended for consumption within her borders without payment of an import duty to themselves. This injustice was long remembered. There were other sufferings greater than the paralysis of trade. There was not a county in the State which was not at some time overrun by the enemy, carrying with them devastation and ruin. And still more terrible, her defenceless homes were exposed to the merciless savages, armed and incited by the ruthless policy of Great Britain. The traditions of these sufferings have been handed down among our people, and form the thrilling incident of legend and of song.

After the return of Carleton to Quebec, Burgoyne, whose ambition was not satisfied with a secondary command, obtained in December a leave of absence and returned to England, where he was sure of court favor. Of obscure and probably illegitimate birth, he had allied himself by a runaway match with Lady Stanley, a daughter of the Earl of Derby. Immediately on his arrival he offered his services to the King in a personal interview, and submitted his views in a paper, entitled "Thoughts for Conducting the War from the side of Canada," on the 28th of February, 1777. In this plan we find for the first time a thoroughly devised scheme for the junction of the Canadian army with that of General Howe. The Canada army, operating from Ticonderoga, was to take possession of Albany, and after opening communication with New York, to remain upon the Hudson River, and thereby enable Howe to act with his whole force to the southward. The plan included a diversion by the Mohawk, and a rising of the loyalists in that region by means of an expedition under the command of Lieutenant-Colonel St. Leger. The King's remarks upon this plan still exist in the original document, in his handwriting in the British Museum. His criticism of it shows strong common sense, and a thorough knowledge of the field of action in America. The point which will be found of most interest is his urgent recommendation "that possession should be taken of Lake George." Nothing, he says, "but an absolute impossibility of succeeding in this can be an excuse for proceeding by South Bay and Skenesborough," which Burgoyne had suggested as an alternative. With regard to the Indians, the King says that "they must be employed."

The order of the campaign being definitely arranged, Lord Germain addressed instructions to General Carleton, on the 20th March, and the next day Burgoyne left London for Plymouth to take passage for Canada. He arrived at Quebec on the 6th May. Carleton immediately put under his command the troops destined for the expedition and committed to his management the preparatory arrangements. Before he left Plymouth Burgoyne had advised Sir William Howe of his purpose to effect a junction with him, and he also sent him a second letter to the same effect from Quebec. On the 10th June he issued his orders for the general disposition of the army at St. John. The movements of the troops were somewhat delayed by bad weather and bad roads, but notwithstanding all impediments the army of invasion assembled between the 17th and 20th June at Cumberland Point, near the foot of Lake Champlain. On the 21st he held a conference with the Indian tribes at the camp on the River Bouquet. Burgoyne, with the main body, reached Crown Point on the 27th June.

Many accounts have been written of the picturesque appearance of the brilliant array of the British army as it passed up the lake. That of Captain Thomas Anburey, an educated young officer in the British service, and an eye-witness of the scenes he described, deserves repetition. "It moved," he says, "by brigades, gradually advancing from seventeen to twenty miles a day, and regulated in such a manner that the second brigade should take the encampment of the first, and so on, each successively filling the ground the other quitted. The time for departure was always at daybreak." The spectacle the enthusiastic young gentleman portrays as one of the most pleasing he ever beheld. "When in the widest part of the lake it was remarkably fine and clear, not a breeze stirring, when the whole army appeared at one view in such perfect regularity as to form the most complete and splendid regatta ever beheld. In the front the Indians went in their birch canoes, containing twenty or thirty in each ; then the advanced corps in a regular line with the gun-boats ; then followed the Royal George and Inflexible, towing large booms, which are to be thrown across two points of land, with the other brigs and sloops following ; after them the brigades in their order." On the 30th Burgoyne issued his famous order : " This army embarks to-morrow to approach the enemy. The services required of this particular expedition are critical and conspicuous. During our progress occasions may occur in which nor difficulty nor labor nor life are to be regarded. This army must not retreat." An advanced corps, under command of General Fraser, was ordered up the west shore of the lake to a point four miles from Ticonderoga, and the German reserve, under Lieutenant-Colonel Breyman, moved up the eastern shore.

On the 1st July the whole army made a movement forward, encamping in two lines, the right wing at the four mile point, the left nearly opposite, on the east shore. Two frigates with gun-boats lay at anchor, covering the lake from the east to the west shores. Just beyond cannon-shot lay the American batteries. The effective strength of the army of invasion at this period is precisely known. Burgoyne himself stated it to have been on the 1st July, the day before he encamped before Ticonderoga, at 7,390 men, exclusive of artillery. These were composed of: British rank and file 3,724, German rank and file, 3,016 ; in all 6,740 regulars ; Canadians and provincials, about 250 ; Indians about 400 ; the artillerymen numbered 473. The total force was therefore 7,863 men. The field train consisted of forty-two pieces, and was unusually complete in all its details. Burgoyne in his narrative complained that the force of Canadians, which was estimated in the plan at 2,000, did not exceed •150 ; a significant circumstance, as showing the correctness of the American estimate of the temper of the province. Of the discipline of the British and German troops nothing need be said ; they were all drilled and experienced soldiers. Among their officers were many who thoroughly understood the service in which they were engaged and the topography of the country in which they were to act. Burgoyne had served with credit, and had distinguished himself by his dash and gallantry in Portugal, and had also the knowledge acquired in Canada the year previous. Major-General Phillips, who commanded the artillery, had won high praise at Minden. Brigadier-General Fraser, who led the picked corps of light troops, had taken part in the expedition against Louisburg and was with Wolfe at Quebec, He also had served in the Canada campaign of 1776. Riedesel was an accomplished officer, carefully trained in the service of the Duke of Brunswick, and had been selected by him to command the German contingents, with the rank of major-general.

The territory threatened by this formidable invasion was again at this period under the sole control of Major-General Schuyler, Congress, on the 22d May, on the recommendation of the Board of War, having resolved that Albany, Ticonderoga, Fort Stanwix, and their dependencies, should form the Northern Department, with General Schuyler in command. Vague reports of the movements of Burgoyne reached Schuyler toward the middle of June, and he at once visited Ticonderoga to look to its defences. No accurate information of the force or designs of the enemy could be obtained, their advance being thoroughly covered by Indian scouts, who either captured or drove in all the reconnoitering parties of the Americans. Nevertheless, it was decided in a council of general officers, held on the 20th June, to defend the post. On the 22d Schuyler returned to Albany to hurry on reinforcements and provisions, leaving the garrison, which consisted of less than twenty-five hundred men, in command of Major-General St. Clair. This was increased by the arrival of nine hundred militia in the course of a few days.

The post at Ticonderoga, notwithstanding its high reputation, was not really tenable. It was overlooked by an eminence known by the name of Sugar Hill, or Mount Defiance, the occupation of which had been neglected, either because of the supposed impracticability of carrying guns to its summit, or of the weakness of the garrison, already spread over an extensive area. St. Clair had expected an attack from the lake side, and had fortified to meet it, but recognized the danger of his situation when on the morning of the 5th the British were seen in possession of Sugar Hill. With his accustomed vigor, General Phillips had ordered a battery of artillery to the top of this eminence, to which the cannon were hoisted from tree to tree. The occupation of Mount Hope by Fraser on the 3d had already cut off the line of retreat by Lake George. There was but one course to pursue—an immediate evacuation of the post and a withdrawal by the only remaining line, that of the lake to Skenesborough. That night part of the cannon were safely embarked on batteaux, those left behind were spiked, and a hasty retreat began ; the sick and the baggage, ordnance and stores, were sent up the lake under charge of Colonel Long, and the main body crossing the lake by the bridge to Mount Independence moved towards Skenesborough by the new road lately cut by the garrison, to which allusion has already been made. The retreat was discovered at daylight on the 6th, and pursuit instantly began. Fraser, taking the route pursued by the garrison with the picket guard, hastened on, closely followed by Riedesel in support, while Burgoyne opened a passage through the bridge and led the galleys in chase of the battery up the lake. The wind being favorable, he overtook the retreating flotilla at Skenesborough, captured two of the covering galleys and compelled the destruction of the batteaux, which were fired by the Americans, who also destroyed the fort and mills at Skenesborough and retired up Wood Creek to Fort Ann. General Burgoyne took post at Skenesborough.

Meanwhile the main body of the Americans under St. Clair, hurrying along the unfinished road through the wilderness, reached Hubbardton, twenty-five miles distant, at one o'clock on the 6th, when a halt was made. At five o'clock, hearing that the rear guard under Colonel Francis, for which he had waited, was coming up, St. Clair, leaving Colonel Warner with one hundred and fifty men at Hubbardton, with orders to follow when they arrived, moved on to Castleton, six miles distant, which he reached at dusk. When Francis joined Warner, they concluded to spend the night at Hubbardton, where they were overtaken the next morning, when on the point of resuming their march, by Fraser's advance The Americans, about twelve hundred in number, formed in a strong position and maintained their ground with spirit until the bugle of the Hessians announced the approach of Riedesel's corps. Their arrival decided the fortune of the day. The Americans behaved with great bravery until overpowered by numbers, when they broke and scattered. The losses in killed and wounded were about equal on the two sides. Fraser led his men in person. Major Grant, an officer of high reputation,

2

was killed.   The Earl of Balcarras, who led the light infantry, and was now for the first time in action, was slightly, and Major Ackland severely, wounded.   Of the Americans, Colonel Francis fell while bravely rallying his men.   St. Clair, hearing of the capture of Skenesborough, struck into the woods on his left.   At Rutland he found some of Warner's fugitives.   Taking a circuitous route, he reached the Hudson River at Batten Kill, and joined General Schuyler at Fort Edward on the 12th.

Schuyler heard on the morning of the 7th, in Albany, rumor of disaster, and immediately started for Fort Edward, to take command of the troops there, and await the arrival of Nixon's brigade from Peekskill, which had been detached from Putnam's command at the Highlands by Washington's orders. At Fort Edward he learned that the party under Colonel Long had turned at Fort Ann and checked the pursuit.   Setting fire to the work, they pushed on to Fort Edward, which they reached on the 9th.   St. Clair, as has been stated, did not come in till the 12th.   The whole force under Schuyler consisted of seven hundred Continental troops and a smaller number of militia, without a single piece of artillery.   St. Clair brought in about fifteen hundred men.   On the 13th Nixon arrived with his brigade of six hundred from Albany, and on the 20th the whole force fit for duty was returned at 4,467 men, half-equipped and deficient in ammunition and every kind of supplies.   Before them, at Skenesborough, within a day's forced march, lay Burgoyne with his superior force of veteran troops, flushed with victory.

The first period of the campaign, as Burgoyne termed it in his narrative of his operations, ended at Skenesborough. So far his march had been successful ; triumphant even. With proud exultation his general orders of the 10th, issued at Skenesborough House, directed that divine service should be performed on the next Sunday at the head of the line and of the advanced corps, and a *feu de joie* to be fired at sunset on the same day with cannon and small arms at Ticonderoga, Crown Point, the camp at Skenesborough,

the camp at Castleton, and the post of Breyman's corps.   In
the hour of pride commenced the second period of Burgoyne's
campaign, which may be termed the period of his errors and
his misfortunes.   In the plan laid before the King, Burgoyne,
as has already been stated, had himself expressed his belief
that the possession of Lake George was of great consequence
as the most expeditious and most commodious route to
Albany, and that by South Bay and Skenesborough should
not be attempted ; and the King himself expressed a similar
opinion, adding that nothing but an absolute impossibility of
succeeding by Lake George should be an excuse for proceeding by the other route.   A glance at the map, even to one
not familiar with the topography of the country, will make
this apparent.   The distance from Ticonderoga to Lake
George is little over two miles.   Lake George itself is about
thirty-five miles long.   The petty naval force on the lake,
consisting of two small schooners, could not have resisted a
brigade of gunboats.   Fort George could have opposed no
serious obstacle to the conqueror of " Ty."

Gordon says, on military authority, and adds that Gates,
who was familiar with every inch of ground, had repeatedly
expressed the same opinion, that by a rapid movement with
light pieces Burgoyne could have reached Albany by the
time he got to the Hudson.   This view was corroborated by
Captain Bloomfield, of the Royal Artillery.   In evidence
before the committee of the House of Commons on the conduct of the campaign, he said that the artillery could have
been easily moved by land from Fort George to the Hudson
River in two days.   Even when at Skenesborough the true
policy of Burgoyne was an immediate return to Ticonderoga
to avail of the water line.   His orders were to move by the
most expeditious route.   But General Burgoyne had pro-
claimed, " This army must not retreat," and Phillips, his
chief adviser, is known to have held the Americans in great
contempt.   Jefferson said of him, of personal knowledge,
" that he was the proudest man of the proudest nation on
earth."   It has been said further that Burgoyne was misled

by Mr. Skene, who had persuaded him of a rising of the loyalists in the region ; and of Skene, that his main object was to secure the building of a military road through the extensive property of which he was proprietor, and which bore his name. Skenesborough is the present Whitehall. ✓

Burgoyne, in excuse for his delays, says that, from the nature of the country and the necessity of waiting a fresh supply of provisions, it was impossible to follow the quick retreat of the Americans, and considered the short cut from Fort Ann to Fort Edward, though attended with great labor, as the most available route. Here was the first great error, of which the alert Schuyler, to whom every inch of the ground was familiar, was quick to take advantage. Immediately upon the arrival of Nixon's Brigade at Fort Edward it was advanced to Fort Ann to fell trees into Wood Creek. and upon the road from Fort Ann south. So thoroughly was this effected that the invading army was compelled to remove at every ten or twelve yards great trees which lay across the road, and exclusive of the natural difficulties of the country, the watery ground and marshes were so numerous that they were compelled to construct no less than forty bridges (one of which was nearly two miles in length) on the march from Skenesborough to Fort Edward. Lake George was partially used for the transport of stores, Fort George, at the head of the lake, having been abandoned by the Americans, who, after saving forty pieces of cannon and fifteen tons of gunpowder, barely escaped being cut off by the movement of the enemy to Fort Edward. Such were the obstructions thrown in his way that Burgoyne only made his headquarters at Fort Edward on the 30th of July, having consumed twenty-four days after his arrival at Skenesborough in a movement of twenty-six miles. Here his eyes were cheered with a first view of the Hudson, a vision delusive as a mirage.

Schuyler, having secured his artillery, began to fall back and, on the 27th, abandoned Fort Edward to the British, taking post at Moses' Creek, four miles below, which Kosciusko had settled upon as a more defensible place than Fort

Edward, which was almost in ruins.   So elated was Schuyler by the bringing off of the artillery, that he wrote that " he believed the enemy would not see Albany this campaign." A week later, by advice of all the general officers, he moved his army, first to Fort Miller, six miles below, then to Saratoga, and finally to Stillwater, about thirty miles north of Albany, where he proposed to await reinforcements and fortify a camp.   Stillwater was reached on the 3d of August, and an intrenchment was begun the next day.

The fall of Ticonderoga had excited intense alarm throughout the country ; the popular imagination had invested it with the impregnability of an enchanted castle.   Its capture had been the first conquest of the patriots, and it was supposed to be the natural key to the Northern region.   Yet in spite of the popular discouragement, the leaders were still hopeful of a happy result of the campaign.   So confident was Schuyler in ultimate success that he expressed the presentiment on the 14th of July that " we shall still have a Merry Christmas," and on the 25th he wrote to the Committee of Albany that the progress of Burgoyne need give no alarm—to use his own words, that should he ever get as far down as Half Moon he would run himself into the greatest danger, and that in all probability his whole army would be destroyed.   This hopefulness was not confined to Schuyler.   Washington himself at this period expressed his opinion that the success Burgoyne had met with "would precipitate his ruin," and that his " acting in detachments was the course of all others most favorable to the American cause."   He adds : " Could we be so happy as to cut one of them off, supposing it should not exceed four, five or six hundred men, it would inspirit the people and do away with much of their present anxiety.   In such an event they would lose sight of past misfortune, and, urged at the same time by a regard for their own security, they would fly to arms and afford every aid in their power."   In view of the events about to transpire, the words of the great chief seem almost prophetic.

To us in these days, looking over the field without passion, prejudice or fear, it seems that even a junction between Burgoyne and Howe would not have been by any means fatal to the patriot cause. The British had not the force adequate to maintain the line of the Hudson. At no time did their army at the north hold more than the ground on which they stood. Howe, like Burgoyne, derived his provisions and supplies from England.

While Burgoyne was slowly plodding his way against almost insuperable difficulties in the path he had chosen, checking desertion only by constant executions, and even by authority to the savages to scalp every soldier found outside the lines, St. Leger, with his command reinforced by Sir John Johnson and the loyalists of Tryon county, appeared before Fort Stanwix on the 2d of August. The story of the siege and the bloody struggle on the field of Oriskany need not be recited here. The brave resistance of the garrison under Gansevoort and Willett, and the heroic behavior of Herkimer and the yeomanry of Tryon against desperate odds, have lately been occasion of centennial celebration. This expedition was a principal feature of the original plan of the campaign, and, although St. Leger held an independent command, his failure was a complete paralysis of the right wing of the army of invasion. Stunned by the resistance he encountered, and learning of the reinforcement of the Americans by troops from Schuyler's command, he retraced his steps to Oswego, and thence with the remnant of his force to Montreal, where he arrived too late to take any further part in the campaign.

From the 30th of July to the 15th of August, Burgoyne was busy at Fort Edward, getting down batteaux, provisions, and ammunition from Fort George to the Hudson, a distance of about sixteen miles. The roads were out of repair in some parts, steep and much broken by exceeding heavy rains; with all his exertions he was not able in fifteen days to accumulate more than four days' provisions for a forward movement. This delay, however, enabled him to carry out anther cherished plan, that of detaching a corps from his left,

in order, to use his own words, "to give jealousy" to Connecticut, and hold in check the country known as the Hampshire Grants.   To this he had been further incited by Major-
General Riedesel, who had commanded the Black Hussars in
Germany, and was now anxious to mount his dragoons.

Besides this inducement, Burgoyne had learned that Bennington was the great deposit of corn, flour, and cattle, that it
was guarded by militia only, and that the country about was
much disaffected to the Americans.   Under these impres-
sions, with this purpose, and being now ready for his own
advance, he despatched an expedition under Lieutenant-
Colonel Baum.   At daybreak on the 14th, Burgoyne broke
camp at Fort Edward and began his advance.   His objective
point was Albany, where he expected to be joined by St.
Leger coming down the Mohawk, and Baum from his raid
upon Bennington.

On the 14th, he established his headquarters at Duer's
house (at Fort Miller), about six miles below.   A bridge of
rafts was constructed, over which the advance corps passed
the Hudson and encamped on the heights of Saratoga.   On
the 17th, before the main body could be gotten over, the
river being swollen by heavy rains, and the current running
rapidly, the bridge was carried away.   The advance being
thus isolated, was recalled, and recrossed the river in scows
and took up their old encampment on the Batten Kill.
Here, at a shoal part of the river, a pontoon was constructed
across the Hudson, directly opposite Saratoga, which was
completed about the 20th.   But obstacles of another nature
presented themselves.   On the 17th, Burgoyne receiving information of disaster to Baum, and suddenly convinced of
the impossibility of obtaining provisions and supplies from
the country, in his general orders informed the troops of
the necessity of a halt.   For the first time his eyes were
opened to the difficulties of his situation.   He found himself
with an extended line of communication, no hope of obtaining provisions in the neighborhood, deceived as to the senti-
ment of the country and in the midst of a hardy population

exulting in success. The surprise and defeat of Baum by Stark and Warner with the New England militia on the 15th of August was not to him the most discouraging feature of the battle of Bennington. It was the rally of the farmers from every quarter, all accustomed to the use of firearms from childhood in a section of country abounding in game. Not Braddock himself in the toils of Indian stratagem was more helpless than the Hessians of Baum and Breyman, with clumsy accoutrements, their heavy boots sinking at every step deep in the wet soil, and moving with military discipline, exposed to the fire of a thousand marksmen concealed by bushes and trees.

To relate the incidents of the glorious victory at this time and before this audience would be to tell a " twice-told tale." But it is not to be forgotten that this battle also was fought on the soil of the Empire State. Its result justified Washington's military judgment in his opinion of the danger to Burgoyne of detached operations, and the enthusiasm it aroused realized his prediction and showed his thorough knowledge of the temper of the people. To the army of Burgoyne the consequences were serious. The return of the scattered remnant of the force, which went out from camp in such high hopes and spirits, damped the ardor of both officers and men. A few days later a courier from St. Leger, guided by a friendly Indian by Saratoga Lake and Glens Falls, brought intelligence of failure in that quarter. The shadow which had fallen on the army now deepened into gloom. In spite of all these discouragements the proud spirit of Burgoyne could not brook the thought of abandoning the expedition. Choosing to adopt a strict construction of the King's orders " to go to Albany," he assumed the entire responsibility of further advance without consultation of his officers.

It was not until the 12th September that Burgoyne, compelled to depend wholly upon Canada for supplies, had accumulated the thirty days' provisions which he thought necessary to his further advance. On that day he issued his orders to move.

His army crossed the Hudson on the 13th, and on the 14th encamped on the heights and plains of Saratoga. Here was the country seat of General Schuyler, with his commodious dwelling, his mill, a church and several houses. Not a living creature was to be seen, but broad fields, rich with waving grain ready for the reaper. Before night the wheat was cut and threshed and in the mill for grinding. The Indian corn was apportioned as forage for the horses, and the beautiful plantation, which in the morning was a scene of peace and plenty, stripped to the last blade. The passage of the river was the close of what Burgoyne terms the second period of his campaign.

Before entering on the third period, which may be termed the battle period, we must return to the American army, which we left under Schuyler at Stillwater, intrenching their camp on the 4th August. On the same day he received advice of the investment of Fort Stanwix ; on the 7th reports of the battle of Oriskany, with exaggerated account of the American loss. On the 11th he detached General Learned to the assistance of the garrison, and on the 15th Arnold, whom Washington had ordered to the Northern Department, because of his encouraging presence to the dispirited militia, was sent up with full powers to cover the Mohawk settlements. Alarmed by the prospect of St. Leger's descent by the Mohawk River, Schuyler, who on every occasion displayed strategic skill of the first order, fell back from Stillwater to the confluence of the Hudson and the Mohawk, where, on the 14th, he took post on Van Schaick's Island, nine miles from Albany. This had been selected as a secure position for the main body, which had been greatly weakened by the detachments sent up the valley of the Mohawk and to the Hampshire Grants, where General Lincoln had gone, by order of Washington, to organize a movement to cut off Burgoyne's communication with Canada.

Correct as all these movements of General Schuyler appear to us now, as seen in the light of history, they were the cause of intense dissatisfaction to the people, whom each successive movement of Burgoyne had filled with alarm. Rumors derogatory to the personal courage and integrity, as well as the patriotism, of Schuyler were rife in all sections, particularly in New England, where the old prejudice against their Dutch neighbors still prevailed.   In all the difficulties with regard to boundary Schuyler had been prominent in defence of the rights of the New York colony, and the antagonism between the two sides of the river was now intensified by the revolt of the Hampshire Grants against the authority of New York, and their declared purpose to set up a State for themselves. Schuyler, whose spirit was high and whose nature was sensitive to excess, chafed sorely under the accusations against him, but, sustained by his own sense of the value of his services, the sympathy of the New York Government and the confidence of Washington, he had maintained his command. The year before he had demanded an investigation into his conduct in evacuating Crown Point, which was looked upon as the beginning of disaster, and had tendered his resignation to Congress, who, however, refused to accept of it, and promised an investigation of his conduct.   In November he had applied again to Congress for permission to repair to Philadelphia on that business, to which Congress consented.   Appointed delegate to Congress by the New York Convention, he had taken his seat in April, and secured the passage of a resolution of inquiry.   The committee made a report in May, which thoroughly vindicated him and placed him in full command of the Northern Department.

The advance of Burgoyne, penetrating into the heart of the country, and the fact that Schuyler himself had personally participated in no engagement, revived the distrust with which he was viewed by the Eastern troops ; a distrust which paralyzed his influence and made a change in the command of the Northern Department an absolute necessity.   No stronger proof of the existence and strength of this feeling is needed than his own words.   Writing to Washington from Saratoga, on the 28th July, he said : " So far from the militia that are with me increasing, they are daily diminishing, and I am very confident that in ten days, if the enemy should not disturb us, we shall not have five hundred left ; and although I have entreated *this* and the Eastern States to send up a re-enforcement of them, yet I doubt much if any will come up when the spirit of malevolence knows no bounds, and I am considered as a traitor."

On the 1st of August Congress passed resolutions ordering General Schuyler to repair to headquarters, and directed Washington to order such general officer as he deemed proper to relieve him in his command. On the 4th a letter from Washington was laid before Congress, asking to be excused from making an appointment of an officer to command the Northern army. An election was then held by Congress, and Major-General Gates was chosen by the vote of eleven States. Washington was informed of the result, and was directed to order General Gates at once to his post. Washington was then at Philadelphia, and the same day informed Gates of his appointment. Schuyler was at Albany when the resolution reached him on the 10th. His magnanimity on this occasion is matter of record. Solomon tells us that, " Better is he that ruleth his spirit than he that taketh a city." To no man of whom history, ancient or modern, makes mention can this phrase be more justly applied than to Schuyler. The judgment of Congress as to the propriety of a change is sufficiently shown by Schuyler's own letters to that body on the 15th August, in which he said that he had not been joined by any of the New England militia, and that there were only sixty or seventy on the ground from the State of New York. Whether Schuyler had great military capacity or not is a question which cannot be answered. That he had no opportunity of displaying it on the field is certain ; that he was possessed of the strongest common sense and of that rarest quality in the human mind, the organizing faculty, is beyond doubt. No other man in America could have performed the services which he rendered, and it may certainly be said that they were second only to those of Washington in importance and extent. He continued in command of the troops until the arrival of Gates on the 19th August, to whom he gave the cordial reception of a soldier and a gentleman.

Gates was by no means overjoyed at the responsibility with which he was entrusted. He found the army dejected, although somewhat encouraged by the victory at Bennington. His arrival revived the spirits of the troops, and the precision which he at once introduced into the camp increased their resolution. Words of congratulation and encouragement pressed in upon him from the eastward, and the announcement of the approach of militia from all sections added to the courage of the men.

During the retreat the army had been greatly distressed by the savages in Burgoyne's command, who hung upon the flanks and outposts, and by their merciless cruelty excited an alarm which their real importance by no means justified. Washington, aware of the disadvantage under which the militia lay in their apprehension from this cause, on the 20th dispatched Colonel Morgan to his assistance with his corps of riflemen. This corps of five hundred men was a *corps d'élite*, which had been selected from the entire army for their proficiency in the use of the rifle and the Indian mode of warfare. Gates thanked Washington warmly for this valuable assistance and for his advice concerning the use to be made of them. They arrived on the 23d. To them Gates added two hundred and fifty bayonets, also carefully picked from the line, whom he placed under the command of Major Dearborn, a determined officer.

On the 8th September, the army having been recruited to about 6,000 men, Gates felt strong enough to make a forward movement, and marched to Stillwater, where a line of intrenchments was begun the next day. It was soon found, however, that the extent of low ground was too great to admit of proper defence of the centre and left. A more favorable point was selected, two miles and a half to the northward, where a range of hills, covered by a narrow defile in front and jutting close upon the river, offered an admirable defensive position. The fortification was at once begun, under the direction of Kosciusko, the Engineer-in-Chief, and the army took possession on

the 12th.   The ground is that which was then and is now
known as Bemis' Heights, and upon it were contested the
hard-fought actions which determined the campaign.   Here
Gates resolved to await the attack of Burgoyne, without pre-
cipitating movements with his mostly raw troops until they had
acquired some discipline ; certainly not until he should hear of
the success of the attempt making to reach Burgoyne's rear
and distress his army.

General Lincoln, who was charged with this expedition,
moved from Manchester to Pawlet with his militia force, consisting of about two thousand men.   On his advance, the
British guard at Skenesborough fell back, destroying a number of boats.   On the 13th he despatched Colonel Brown with
five hundred men to the landing at Lake George, to release
the American prisoners and destroy the British stores, and the
same number of men under Colonel Johnson to Mount Independence, to create a diversion in favor of the operations of
Colonel Brown, who was directed to push to Ticonderoga, if
opportunity offered.   A like number of men was also sent,
under Colonel Woodbridge, to Skenesborough, thence to
Fort Ann, and on to Fort Edward.   Lincoln at once advised
Gates of this movement.   Colonel Brown managed his operations with great skill and secrecy.   After a night march he
reached the north end of Lake George at daybreak on the
morning of the 17th, surprising in detail all the outposts between the landing and the fortress of Ticonderoga ; Mount
Defiance, Mount Hope, the French lines, a block-house, two
hundred batteaux and several gunboats, taking prisoners two
hundred and ninety-three British and Canadians, and releas-
ing one hundred Americans.   Among his trophies was the
Continental standard left at Ty when the Fort was evacuated.
The guns at Fort Defiance were turned upon the fortress of
Ticonderoga, but no impression could be made on its walls.
Taking the gunboats, Brown sailed up the lake, and on the
24th made an attack on Diamond Island, about four miles
north of Fort George, but was warmly received and repulsed.
Making for the eastern shore, he reached the camp of General

Warner at Skenesborough on the 26th, by way of Fort Ann. A curious testimony to the effect of these raids on thé rear of the British army exists in the Gates papers, in an intercepted letter from St. Leger, written at Ticonderoga the 29th September, informing Burgoyne of his arrival there, and asking for guides to lead him down.

To return to Burgoyne, whom we left encamped at Saratoga on the 14th. The next day he moved forward at noon, forming his troops into three columns, after passing Schuyler's house, and encamped at Dovogat (the present Coeville), where they lay accoutred that night. On the 16th there was a fog so heavy that even foragers were forbidden to leave camp. Later in the day detached parties were employed in repairing the bridges and reconnoitering the country.

On the 17th the army resumed their march, repaired bridges and encamped at Sword's Farm, four miles from Gates' position. The general orders directed the army to be under arms at an hour before daybreak. His approach was known to Gates by report of his adjutant, Wilkinson, who led a scouting party and saw the passage of the river. On the 18th preparations were made to harass him, and General Arnold was sent out with fifteen hundred men to endeavor to stop the repair of the bridges. After some light skirmishing Arnold fell back, and Burgoyne moved forward as far as Wilbur's Basin, about two miles from the American position. He there established his camp, which he fortified with intrenchments and redoubts, his left on the river, his right extending at right angles to it across the low ground about six hundred yards, to a range of steep and lofty heights ; a creek or gully in his front, made by a rivulet which issued from a great ravine formed by the hills, known as the North Ravine.

On the morning of the 19th, Burgoyne, after a careful reconnoitering of the passages of the great ravine and the road around its head, leading to the extreme left of the American camp, advanced to the attack in three divisions. Fraser on the right, with the light infantry, sustained by Breyman's German riflemen, and covered on the flanks by Canadians, Provincials, and Indians, made a wide circuit to the west in order to pass the ravine without quitting the heights, and afterwards to cover the march of the line to the right. The centre, commanded by Burgoyne in person, passed the ravine in a direct line south, and formed in order of battle as fast as they gained the summit, where they waited to give time for Fraser to make the circuit. The left wing, led by Riedesel and Phillips, and composed of the Hessian troops and the artillery, moved along the river road and meadows in two columns. Their advance was delayed by the repair of the bridges. The Forty-seventh Regiment were charged with the guard of the batteaux containing the stores of the army. Burgoyne's purpose was himself to attack the left of the American lines in front and engage their attention until Fraser, moving over the table land, should turn the extreme left of the American position and reach their rear. Riedesel and Phillips were to change direction at the southern end of the ravine and march west to connect with the British centre. When, between one and two o'clock, the columns had reached their positions they moved at signal guns. From the conformation of the ground this was the only practicable manner by which Burgoyne could possibly advance, the river road being covered by the American artillery.

Beyond the great North Ravine in front of the British position, and half way between it and the ground fortified by the Americans, there was another deep ravine called the Middle Ravine, through which Mill Creek still runs, and directly in front of the American camp and covered by its guns was another ravine of lesser extent, but still a formidable obstruction to the advance of an enemy. The whole country, with the exception of a few cleared patches, was heavily wooded, the ravines as well as the upper table lands. On the high ground (Bemis' Heights) south was the American entrenched line, extending eastwardly to the river bank and westwardly to the extremity of the hill where a redoubt was begun. Beyond it felled trees obstructed the passage of the gullies between the flank defences on the left and the neighboring hills. The lines, which were about a mile in extent, enclosed what is still known as Neilson's Farm. The hills on the east of the Hudson commanded a general view of Burgoyne's camp.

On the morning of the 19th, Gates was informed by Lieutenant-Colonel Colburn, of the New Hampshire line, who had been sent out the day before to observe the movements of the enemy, that the British had struck their tents and crossed the gully at the gorge of the great ravine, and were ascending the heights toward the American left. Arnold, who commanded the left wing, and was at this time at headquarters, suggested a movement to attack. Colonel Morgan, with his rifle corps, supported by Major Dearborn's light infantry, was immediately ordered out to observe their direction and harass their advance. About half-past twelve a report of small arms announced that Morgan's men had struck the enemy. They had fallen in with Burgoyne's pickets, who made the advance guard of the British line, and had posted themselves in a cabin on Freeman's farm, which was one of the few cleared spots in that thickly wooded country. They were quickly dislodged by Morgan, who, pursuing hotly, fell on the main body, which Burgoyne had formed into line in the first opening in the woods, by whom they were instantly routed, with loss of several officers and men. Wilkinson, who witnessed the rally of the riflemen, hurried to Gates, who at once gave directions for their support. Cilley's and Scammel's regiments of New Hampshire (part of General Poor's brigade of Continental regulars) were ordered to advance through the woods and take ground on the left of Morgan, and the action was renewed about one o'clock.

This movement would have turned the British right but for the disposition of General Fraser, who had promptly arrived at his appointed post and taken an advantageous position on a height, which covered the British right. Meeting this obstacle the Americans counter-marched, and pushed through the woods toward the left of Burgoyne's column. To their

support the five remaining regiments of Poor's brigade, consisting of Hale's, of New Hampshire ; Van Cortlandt's and
Henry Livingston's, of New York, and Cook's and Latimer's,
of the Connecticut Militia, were successively led to the field
at the points of the action where greatest pressure was per-
ceived.   About three o'clock the action became general.   Burgoyne's division was vigorously attacked and suffered severely.
One regiment of grenadiers and part of the light infantry under
Lord Balcarras from Fraser's division participated at times in
the action, but it was not thought advisable to weaken Fraser's force on the heights, except partially and occasionally.
Major-General Phillips, hearing the firing, made his way at
once through the woods to Burgoyne's support, bringing with
him four pieces of artillery, a difficult task, considering the
nature of the ground, and entered the action at a critical time.
Riedesel also got up with part of the left wing before the close
of the battle.   The Americans, feeling the pressure of this
reinforcement, Gates ordered out the whole of Learned's
brigade, consisting of Bailey's, Wesson's, and Jackson's regiments, of the Massachusetts line, and James Livingston's, of
New York, and also Marshall's regiment, of the Massachusetts
line.   They were but slightly engaged.   Darkness ended the
contest, the Americans only withdrawing when objects became
undistinguishable.   The number engaged on each side was
not far from equal.   The American force was about 3,000,
and Burgoyne stated his to be about 3,500.   The mode of
fighting of the Americans more than equalled this discrep-
ancy.   The field of action was such that, although the com-
batants changed ground a dozen times in the course of the
day, the contest terminated with each body in its original position.   The British were formed on an eminence in a thin
pine wood, having before it Freeman's farm, an oblong field,
stretching from its centre toward its right, the ground in
front sloping gently down to the verge of the field, which was
bordered on the opposite side by a close wood, held by the
Americans.   The sanguinary scene lay in the cleared ground
between the eminence occupied by the enemy and the wood

3

just mentioned.   The fire of the American marksmen from the wood was too deadly to be withstood by the British in line, and when they gave way and broke, the Americans, making for their centre, pursued them to the eminence, where, having their flanks protected, they rallied, and charging in turn drove the Americans back into the wood, whence a dreadful fire would again force them to fall back, and in this manner did the battle fluctuate, like the waves of a stormy sea, with alternate advantage, for four hours without one moment's intermission; the British artillery fell into the hands of the Americans at every charge, but they could neither turn the pieces on the enemy nor bring them off; the wood prevented the last, and the want of a match the first, as the linstock was invariably carried off, and the rapidity of the transitions would not allow time to provide one.   The slaughter of the artillery was remarkable, the captain and twenty-six men out of forty-eight being killed or wounded.   Such is Wilkinson's concise and picturesque account of this action, which he considered one of the longest, warmest, and most obstinate battles fought in America.   Here was seen the superiority of the American rifle over the British bayonet, on which Burgoyne so confidently relied.   In his report to Congress, Gates accorded the glory of the action entirely to the valor of the rifle regiment and corps of light infantry under the command of Colonel Morgan.   The British were surprised at the courage and obstinacy with which the Americans fought, and, as one who was present has recorded, found to their dismay that they were not that contemptible enemy they had been hitherto imagined, incapable of standing a regular engagement, and willing only to fight behind strong and powerful works.

The battle on the part of the Americans was essentially a soldiers' battle.   While Burgoyne led his men in person, exposing himself with great bravery, directing the movements of the British line, the Americans had no general officer in the field until the evening, when General Learned was ordered out.   The battle was fought by the general concert and zealous co-operation of the corps engaged, and sustained more by individual courage than military discipline, as is shown by the loss of the militia in comparison with that of the regular troops.

During the action Gates and Arnold remained in front of the centre of the camp. This is no matter for comment or surprise, as it was neither the policy nor the purpose of Gates to bring on a general engagement, which might have involved his forces to such an extent as to leave his right exposed and uncover the river road. The intrenchments were not half completed, those on the left hardly begun. Moreover, the militia were every day arriving. Each day's delay increased his own chances of success while diminishing those of the enemy.

The loss of the Americans, killed, wounded and missing, was three hundred and twenty-one; that of the British, six hundred—a disparity more remarkable, as the ground did not admit of the use of artillery by the Americans. Both sides claimed the victory; in reality it was a drawn battle. The British held the strong position Fraser had occupied in the morning, which, however, Gates had no desire of disputing, as his army was acting on the defensive. The Americans, on the other hand, had marched out from their camp, met the enemy more than half way, and after inflicting upon them a stunning blow, returned to their intrenchments. Far more important than any physical advantage was the effect on the *morale* of the two armies. The patriots had met the main body of the invading army on equal terms, while the invaders had learned to their bitter cost the terrors of a warfare in which their discipline was of little avail.

The British lay on their arms the night of the battle, and the next day, the 20th, took a position just out of reach of the cannon of the American camp, where they fortified, and at the same time extended their left to the brow of the heights, so as to cover the meadows on the river. A bridge of boats was thrown over the Hudson, and a work erected on the east

side of the river.   The Americans on their side worked dili-
gently in completing the defences of their extremely strong
position.   The morning was foggy, and there was consider-
able alarm in the American camp, caused by the story of a
deserter, that an attack was intended.   It has been since
stated that Burgoyne really directed a movement, but was
dissuaded by General Fraser, who, because of the fatigue of
his men, begged for a day's delay.   Meanwhile a spy from
Clinton brought a letter to Burgoyne, with advice of his
intended expedition against the Highlands, which determined
him to postpone the attack and await events.   If such were
the case, this was another and fatal error of Burgoyne.   His
general orders, however, of the 20th, ordering the advance
of the army at 3 o'clock, seem inconsistent with the story,
and there is no confirmation of it in his own narrative ; but,
on the contrary, he admits that he was persuaded that the
American camp was strongly fortified.   On the 22d, Gates
learned from General Lincoln of Colonel Brown's success at
Ticonderoga.   His reply to Lincoln shows that at this time
he did not feel himself strong enough to prevent Burgoyne's
retreat.   He therefore urged the destruction of all buildings,
batteaux, etc., on the line which should afford him shelter,
that, to use his own words, "he may have no resting-place
until he reaches Canada."   The next morning he adds a
postscript, to the effect that, by his scouts, it was "past a
doubt that the enemy's army remain in their camp, that their
advance was within one mile of his own, and urged the
immediate forwarding of the militia."   He is satisfied, he adds,
"that New York, and not Ticonderoga, is General Burgoyne's
object."

On the 23d, in consequence of a direction in general orders
that Morgan's independent corps was responsible to headquarters only, a difference which had been long brewing
between Gates and Arnold ended in a public dispute.   High
words passed between them.   Arnold was excluded from
headquarters, and demanded permission to go to Philadelphia
to report to Congress, a request of which Gates took instant

advantage. Suspended from command at his own desire, Arnold found too late the unfortunate position in which he would place his reputation by leaving the army at this critical juncture. He changed his mind and remained in camp, murmuring discontent and spreading sedition by the intemperance of his conduct and language. Gates took Arnold's division under his own command and assigned Lincoln, who came in the same day, to the command of the right wing.

With the militia who flocked to Gates' camp came a band of Oneida and Tuscarora Indians, who had been persuaded by the influence of Schuyler, then active as Indian Commissioner, to join the army. They were objects of such curiosity that it became necessary to forbid the soldiers from flocking to their encampment. These Indians were, however, a terror to the enemy. Gates' orders distinguished them from Burgoyne's savages by a red woollen cap.

On the 3d October, Burgoyne was compelled to diminish the soldiers' rations, the foraging parties meeting but little success, and requiring heavy covering parties. The Americans were constantly in the field, harassing the advanced pickets, and night alarms prevented the British from quitting their clothes and deprived them of rest. The main bodies of both armies lay in quiet, while the woods resounded to the stroke of the axe, felling trees for the fortifications. Burgoyne sent word to Clinton on the 23d September, that he would await news from him until the 12th October.

Riedesel, in his memoirs of the campaign, says that the situation becoming daily more critical and the enemy too strong, both in numbers and position, to be attacked, Burgoyne on the 4th called Generals Phillips, Riedesel, and Fraser, to consult with them as to what measures to adopt. He proposed to leave the boats and stores under strong guard, and turning the left wing of Gates, to attempt an attack ; no decision was arrived at. A second conference was held on the evening of the 6th, when Riedesel recommended an immediate attack or a return to Batten-Kill. Fraser approved of this plan. Phillips declined to express an opinion. Burgoyne terminated the discussion by declaring that he would make a reconoissance of the left wing of the Americans on the 7th, and if there were any prospect of success he would attack on the 8th or return to a position at Freeman's Farm, and on the 11th begin a retreat to the rear of Batten-Kill.

Just before noon on the 7th Burgoyne marched out of camp with fifteen hundred men and ten pieces of artillery, destined for the reconnoissance, and also to cover a foraging party to relieve their immediate distress. The troops were formed into three columns, under Phillips, Riedesel, and Fraser, within three-quarters of a mile of the American left. The rangers, Indians, and provincials, were ordered to pass through the woods and gain the rear of the camp. The foraging party entered a field and began to cut the wheat in sight of the American outposts, when the alarm was given and the Americans beat to arms. Wilkinson went to the front to see the cause, and observed the foragers at work, the covering party, and the officers with their glasses endeavoring to reconnoitre the American left. He reported their position to Gates and gave as his opinion that they were inclined to offer battle. "I would indulge them," he added, whereupon Gates replied : "Well, then, order on Morgan to begin the game." A plan was concerted, with the approval of Gates, for Morgan to make a detour and gain a height on the right of the enemy, time enough for which was allowed him before Poor's brigade were sent to attack the left. The British generals were still consulting as to the best mode of pursuing the reconnoissance when the New Hampshire and New York troops of Poor's Brigade fell upon the British left, where the grenadiers under Major Ackland were posted, with impetuous fury and extended the attack to the front of the Germans. At this time Morgan descended the hill and striking the light infantry on the right endeavored to turn their flank. Seeing his danger of being enveloped, Burgoyne ordered a second position to be taken by the light infantry to secure the return of his troops to camp. Meanwhile Poor's brigade pressed the left with ardor and compelled them to give way. Fraser, with part of his light infantry, moved rapidly to prevent an entire rout, and fell mortally wounded. Phillips and Riedesel were then ordered to cover a general retreat, which was effected in good order, though hard pressed, the enemy leaving eight pieces of cannon in the hands of the Americans, most of their artillerymen being killed or wounded.

Hardly had the British entered their camp when it was stormed with great fury in the face of a severe fire of grape and musketry. The British intrenchments were stoutly defended by Balcarras and no impression was made. The German entrenched camp of Breyman, with the provincials, was carried by Learned, who appeared on the ground with his fresh brigade at sunset, and an opening was thus made in the right and rear which exposed the whole British camp, but the darkness of the night, and the fatigue and disorder of the men, prevented advantage being taken of this situation.

In the night Burgoyne broke up his camp and retired to his original position, which he had fortified behind the Great Ravine. Thus closed the second battle of Saratoga, known as the Battle of Bemis Heights. The loss of the British was estimated at six hundred killed, wounded and taken prisoners, that of the Americans did not exceed one hundred and fifty killed and wounded. Burgoyne lost the flower of his officers. Besides General Fraser and Sir Francis Clark, his principal aide, who were mortally wounded, and Breyman who was killed, Majors Ackland and Williams were taken prisoners, the former wounded. On the American side Arnold, who behaved with the most desperate valor, exposing himself in a frantic manner and leading the troops without authority, just as the victory was won received a ball which fractured his leg and killed his horse ; and General Lincoln, while on his way to order a cannonade on the enemy's camp, received a musket-ball in the leg which shattered the bone. With regard to the conduct of this battle, much has been said. Gates has been blamed for not leaving his camp, and Arnold has been lauded as the hero of the day. These criticisms are equally unjust. Up to sunset, when Learned's corps was sent

forward to finish the action, there was only one brigade in
the field.   Gates' place was with the centre and right, where
the militia were posted, and the security of his camp and the
protection of the road to Albany his one true concern.   Arnold's reckless daring no doubt encouraged and inspired the
troops, but there is no evidence of any generalship on his part.
Had the day resulted differently, he would have been deser-
vedly cashiered.   Gates, in his report to Congress of the
12th, with great magnanimity, mentioned his gallantry and
wound while forcing the enemy's breastworks.   While com-
mending all the troops engaged for their spirit, he gave es-
pecial praise to Morgan's riflemen and Dearborn's light
infantry.

When Burgoyne fell back to his original position, he was
in hopes that this change of front would induce Gates to form
a new disposition, and perhaps attack him in his lines, where
his superior artillery would have given him the advantage.
During the 8th, he repeatedly offered battle to the American
right, but Gates was too thorough a soldier to be tempted in
this manner.   His plans were more comprehensive.   On the
evening of the 7th he ordered General Fellows, who was at
Tift's Mill with thirteen hundred men, to move to a position
to prevent the recrossing of the Hudson at the Saratoga Ford.
On the morning of the 8th Fellows took possession of the
Saratoga barracks and began to throw up intrenchments, and
sent an express to Bennington to hurry up troops to his assistance.   Gates at once took possession of the abandoned
camp at Freeman's Farm.

Burgoyne receiving intelligence of this movement in his
rear, began his retreat at nine o'clock at night, leaving his
sick and wounded.   A heavy rain causing him to delay at
Dovogat, he only reached Saratoga on the night of the 9th,
and his artillery could not pass the ford of the Fishkill till the
morning of the 10th.   On the approach of the advance guard,
Fellows, who had received notice of the retreat, crossed to
the east side of the Hudson, where he was joined by the
militia from Bennington, the rear of which arrived as Bur-

goyne's front reached Saratoga. General Bayley, who commanded the militia column, had posted a force of one thousand men to guard an intermediate ford, and also detached one thousand men to Fort Edward, to the command of which, at the request of Bayley, Stark was assigned on the 14th. The main body of Gates' army, having prepared their provisions and equipped themselves, started in pursuit about noon. In the afternoon of the 10th at four o'clock the advance reached Saratoga, and found Burgoyne encamped on the height beyond the Fishkill. Gates' forces took a position in the wood, on the Saratoga heights, their right resting on the brow of the hill, about a mile in the rear of the Fishkill.

On the 11th Morgan was ordered to cross the Fishkill and fall upon the enemy's rear; there was a heavy fog. Morgan struck their pickets and concluded that Burgoyne had not retired as was supposed. Patterson's and Learned's brigades were ordered to his support, and a vigorous cannonade was opened on the front and rear. Twelve hundred men of Patterson's corps had hardly crossed the creek when the fog lifted and the whole British Army was discovered in line of battle. The Americans fell back over the creek in disorder. Learned's corps was halted and the two brigades retired to a point a half mile distant, where they threw up entrenchments, which they held. The Americans succeeded in destroying a large number of batteaux and stores.

The American artillery, which had taken no active part in the earlier battles, now came into play; the passages of the river were covered by an incessant fire, every attempt to move the batteaux was instantly arrested, and as Burgoyne himself stated, no part of his position was secure from the guns.

On the 12th a council of war was called by Burgoyne, and a retreat, leaving stores and baggage, was agreed upon, but the scouts reporting that no movement could be made without immediate discovery, the project was abandoned. On the 13th, only three days' stores remaining, a second council was held to which all field officers and captains commanding corps were invited. They decided that the situation justified

capitulation upon honorable terms. Negotiations were opened on the 14th with General Gates, and on the 16th the convention was signed. On the 17th October, the British army laid
down its arms on the green in front of old Fort Hardy, on
the north bank of the Fishkill, in the presence of Wilkinson,
Gates' adjutant, and Burgoyne, accompanied by Riedesel
and Phillips, rode to the American headquarters. They
were met by General Gates, followed by his suite, and accompanied by General Schuyler, who had come up from Albany for the occasion. The British troops were then marched
past in view of the American army, whose moderation in the
hour of triumph is one of the most pleasing incidents of this
historic scene. Burgoyne completed the formality of surrender by the tender of his sword.

The total force surrendered, as appears by the official return, signed by General Burgoyne, and preserved among the
Gates papers in the New York Historical Society, was 5,791,
of which 3,379 were English and provincials and 2,412 German auxiliaries, together with a train of artillery of twenty-
seven pieces.

The strength of the American army, rank and file, at Saratoga on the day of surrender, appears from the same doc-
uments to have been 11,098, of which 7,716 of the Continental line [regulars], and 3,382 militia. In reviewing the
whole campaign it will be observed how little real reliance
could be placed on the militia, whose short terms of service
were a source of perpetual anxiety to the General in command. No better or more appropriate illustration of this can
be given than the action of the militia of the Hampshire
Grants, whom General Gates had ordered to his support.
The arrival in camp, on the 18th September, of these victors
of Bennington, under General Stark, the hero of that battle,
animated the whole army, who were aware that they were on
the eve of an engagement, but to the mortification and disgust
of Gates, their term of service expiring the same day, they
marched home from the camp without unpacking their baggage, and as Wilkinson asserts, without any effort to induce

them to remain on the part of their officers. It is not to be denied that the militia did occasional noteworthy service, but the brunt of the engagements fell upon the regular Continen- tal troops, who before the close of the war became in every way the equal of their British foes.

The series of engagements known as the battle of Saratoga has been styled one of the fifteen decisive battles of the world. Its consequences were of such vast importance as to entitle it to this distinction. The long-cherished plan of the British Ministry, pursued through two campaigns with persevering obstinacy, was finally defeated. The open alliance of France was secured ; the United States of America were recognized by the continental powers. The news of the victory spread rapidly over the land, carrying joy to the hearts of the patriots. Washington viewed it as a signal stroke of Provi- dence. Congress voted the thanks of the nation to General Gates and his army, and a gold medal was struck and pre- sented to him in commemoration of the event.

The last days of a century are closing upon these memor- able scenes. How long will it be ere the government of this Empire State shall erect a monument to the gallant men who fought and fell upon these fields and here secured her liberty and renown ?

www.ingramcontent.com/pod-product-compliance
Lightning Source LLC
Chambersburg PA
CBHW030912260626
47169CB00008B/2806